# JAKE AND CLOE
## A TADPOLE AND A POLLYWOG
### The Adventures Begin

WRITTEN BY CHERYL AND DANA HENRICKSEN   ILLUSTRATED BY JEREMY CANIGLIA

CHANNEL PHOTOGRAPHICS / Channel Kids'

980 Lincoln Ave. Ste 200 B   San Rafael, California, 94901
Tel.: 415.456.2934
www.channelphotographics.com

Copyright 2010 Channel Photographics / Channel Kids'

ISBN-13: 978-0-9773399-6-9

US/Canadian Distribution - Publishers Group West
1700 Fourth Street   Berkeley, CA 94710
Tel: 877-528-1444

Text Copyright – Cheryl & Dana Henricksen
Illustrations by Jeremy Caniglia
Edited by Adrianne Casey
Design by Jacqueline Domin, www.jaccadesign.com

Printed and bound in China by Global PSD,
www.globalpsd.com

Channel Photographics & Global Printing, Sourcing & Development
in association with American Forests and the Global ReLeaf programs, will
plant two trees for each tree used in the manufacturing of this book.
Global ReLeaf is an international campaign by American Forests,
the nation's oldest nonprofit conservation organization and a
world leader in planting trees for environmental restoration.

Replanted Paper

In loving memory of my Mom, Judy,
who taught me the important lessons in life.

Cheryl Henricksen

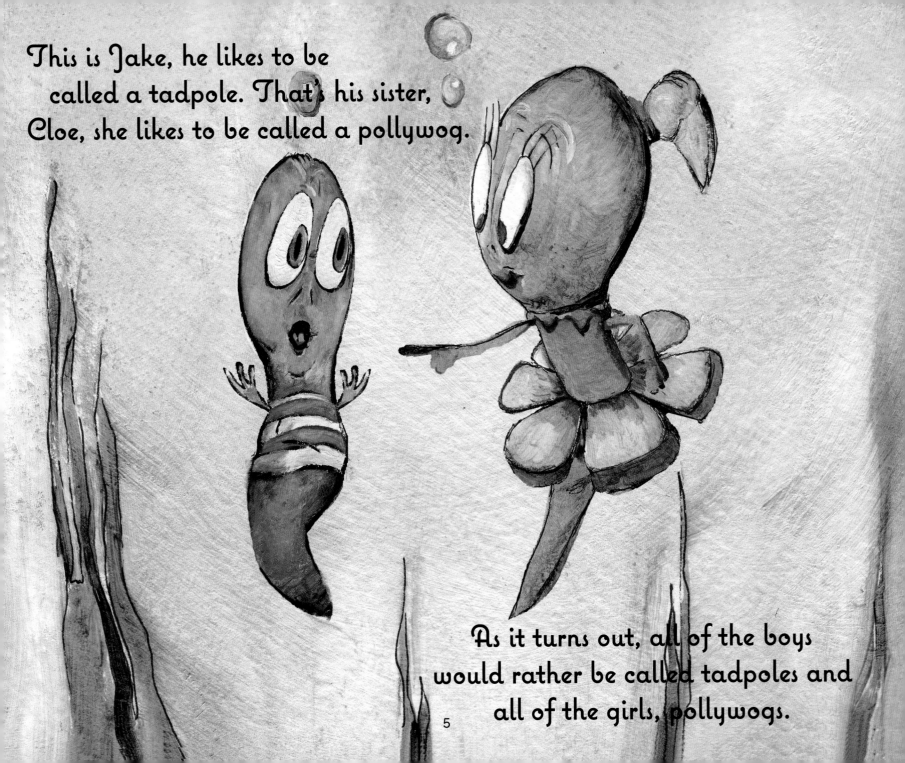

This is Jake, he likes to be called a tadpole. That's his sister, Cloe, she likes to be called a pollywog.

As it turns out, all of the boys would rather be called tadpoles and all of the girls, pollywogs.

Jake and Cloe live in a place called Hoplolly Pond. Hoplolly Pond is low in the valley and surrounded by purple mountains, emerald green hills, and wild flowers that dance in the summer's breeze.

The water in Hoplolly Pond is crystal clear and reflects the beautiful blue sky from above. All kinds of birds and animals enjoy coming to the pond to eat the plants, take a cool drink, bathe in the pond or just play in the water.

Jake has made friends with most of the birds and animals that visit Hoplolly Pond.

He goes to the top of the pond to talk to the animals and play and swim with them in the water.

Many of the tadpoles and
pollywogs do not understand why
Jake plays with the other animals.
After all, Jake is a tadpole,
not a duck or a bird.

Jake's friends find it strange
that he is always going to the top of
the pond, especially on rainy days!

Jake's mother tells him that it is
alright to have many friends, even
if they are not just like you.
There is nothing wrong with being friends
with the birds, rabbits, squirrels and deer.

Maybe the other tadpoles are just
    afraid of the many kinds of animals
and birds, but not Jake.  Jake has many friends.

Jake thinks his sister Cloe is alright most of the time, except when she gets bossy. Jake just plugs his ears and sings when he doesn't want to listen to her anymore.

Cloe thinks that Jake can be annoying. After all, she is the one who has to go find Jake when he does not come home on time. Cloe always knows to look at the top of the pond before looking anywhere else to find her brother.

Most days in Hoplolly Pond are bright and sunny. Only on sunny days will the little tadpoles and pollywogs swim and play close together all around   the pond.

They swim from the bottom of the pond all the way to the top and then from one side to the other.

On rainy days they are all afraid to swim
near the top of the pond and stay close
to the bottom, but not Jake!

One night Jake and Cloe were quietly eating
their supper and Cloe said, "Jake, I think it is going to rain
tomorrow."  Jake became so excited that he
couldn't finish his supper.

Cloe asked Jake, "Why do you like rainy days so much? Nobody likes the rainy days. The raindrops hit the top of the pond and the thunder is so loud that it scares everybody!"

Jake answered, "rainy days are very special to me." "Why are rainy days so special to you?" asked Cloe. Jake replied, "if it does rain tomorrow I will show you."

Jake went to bed that night wishing that it would rain the next day.

Morning came and Jake slowly made his way to the breakfast table. "Jake, do you realize that your wish came true? It is raining right now!" Cloe said.

"Yippee Skippee!!!" hollered Jake.
"Hurry up, we have to leave
right now, please Cloe, we have to go now!
I have to show you why rainy days
are so special to me!"

"Where are we going?" asked Cloe.
"We're going to the top of the pond.
Hurry, we need to Hurry, go faster.
Come On Cloe!" said Jake.

Jake scurried up to the top of the pond
dragging Cloe all the way behind him.
All of the other tadpoles and pollywogs
were swimming down in the other direction,
they seemed to be afraid. They were going to
the bottom of the pond as fast as
they could swim.

As Jake and Cloe were getting closer to the top of the pond Jake could see that the rain was ending and the sun was beginning to peek through the clouds. Again, he yelled to his sister, "We have to go faster!"

As they got to the top of the pond they lifted
their heads out of the water.
Cloe brought along her umbrella just in case
it was still raining.

Cloe looked around the pond and saw rocks and trees
and the animals peeking out of their hiding places.
"I don't see anything special about rainy days, Jake".

"Look!  Look Up!
See, There It Is!"
yelled Jake.

Cloe gasped as
she turned her head
and looked up.  She
was so amazed at
what she was
seeing.  "Oh
my gosh, Jake, it is so
Beautiful!"

"What is it?" Cloe asked.
"It's a Rainbow."
Jake answered with a huge smile.
"This is why rainy days are so special!"

All of the animals came out to see the rainbow as well. The ducks were happily swimming, the birds were sweetly singing and the butterflies were gracefully dancing.

"Remember Cloe to always look for a rainbow after it has rained, that is the Only time you will see it!"

Their parents were always telling Cloe how amazing Jake was. Now Cloe knows for herself just how wonderful Jake really is!